BREAK-IN

at the Basilica

Written by Dianne Ahern
Illustrated by Katherine Larson

AUNT DEE'S ATTIC

Adventures with Sister Philomena,
Special Agent to the Pope:
BREAK-IN AT THE BASILICA

Text © 2006 Dianne M. Ahern
Illustrations © 2006 Katherine Larson

A Book from Aunt Dee's Attic

Published by *Aunt Dee's Attic, Inc.*
415 Detroit Street, Suite 200
Ann Arbor, MI 48104

Printed and bound in Italy

Library of Congress Control Number: 2006901289

ISBN 0-9679437-8-7

1 2 3 4 5 6 7 8 9 10

First Edition

www.auntdeesattic.com

This book is dedicated to the DiGiulio and Tucci families and their Italian heritage.

SPECIAL THANK YOU AND ACKNOWLEDGMENTS TO:

The proofreaders, editors and reviewers who came to the aid of the author, including: Lisa Tucci, Josiah Shurtliff, Shiobhan Kelly, Leo DiGiulio, Joan Copenhaver, Lauren and Kristin Bos, Isabella and Teodoro Napoleone, and LeAnn Fields.

The people who shaped the story, including Delaney and Riley Miner, Austin and Blake Witchie, Julianna Leitch, and Dr. Terry Braciszewski.

Other books by Dianne Ahern and Katherine Larson:

Adventures with Sister Philomena,
Special Agent to the Pope series:
Lost in Peter's Tomb

On the Sacraments:
Today I Was Baptized
Today I Made My First Reconciliation
Today I Made My First Communion
Today We Became Engaged

CHAPTER ONE

THE THEFT

The small man in a shabby green coat and gray trousers tries to make himself as small as possible as he squeezes between the massive wooden choir chairs. It is nightfall and Luigi has come to the Basilica of Saint Francis in Assisi with the intent to steal something of great value.

Luigi is a desperate and poor man. He has no money. His only daughter, whom he loves very much, wants to become a nun, and Luigi wants her to have a dowry to take to the convent when she enters. He is afraid she will be refused entry into the Order unless he can offer the sisters some money or an object of value. God forbid his daughter will have to live forever poor like him.

Several weeks ago he came to the grand Basilica of Saint Francis to pray for an answer to his dilemma. It was then that he discovered a beautiful silver stand tucked away in a display case in a small room near the main altar.

At the time he thought this silver stand would be perfect. The more he thought about it, the more certain he became. The stand looks very special and very

beautiful, like his daughter. It must be quite valuable, because it is in one of the most famous basilicas in the whole world. Then he wonders: why is the silver stand tucked away in a small room like this? Will anyone ever know it's gone?

Luigi tries not to breathe, thinking to himself "I will hide here until the guards leave." Just then, a young man in a black uniform walks past his hideaway.

"Hah! He does not see me here in this dark corner!" Luigi mumbles under his breath. "These young men, these guards, they love their uniforms and the power they think it gives them." Then he thinks about all the money they are paid for doing not much more than telling the tourists to be silent.

"Silenzio!" they shout every few minutes when the tourists get too excited about the beautiful church. Then at closing, the guards strut through the basilica just to be sure all the tourists are gone. He knows this because he has watched their actions for the last two weeks as he has been planning the break-in.

It's at least an hour after the guards leave before Luigi decides to move from his cramped position between the enormous dark wooden chairs. While he was waiting, he ate the small sandwich he brought with him and washed it down with cheap wine from a little cardboard box. The bread, although crumbly, was sweet and a perfect compliment to the salty cheese in his sandwich. Luigi is careful to eat his sandwich over the opening in his rucksack so he doesn't leave any crumbs behind on the floor. "Yes sir, I am a cautious thief," he thinks.

Suddenly a chill runs down his spine. The sunlight that hours ago lit up the stained-glass windows high above his head has long vanished. Now, the light from the full moon casts strange shadows on the pictures painted on the walls of the basilica. Luigi hears the howl of a wolf coming from outside. He feels a burst of warm air brush his cheek. His skin turns all prickly.

"Maybe this isn't such a good idea," he murmurs to himself. But it is too late to turn back.

He pulls a heavy flashlight out of his rucksack. "This should do the trick," he whispers as he slaps the palm of his hand with the handle of the flashlight. *Whap, whap!*

Quietly and carefully he crawls out from between the wooden choir chairs, pulling the empty rucksack behind him. Using his flashlight, Luigi searches for and finds the stairs that lead to the lower part of the basilica. Although it is summer, the coldness and dampness from the stone floor creep into his joints, and he feels an ache in his bones.

The light from Luigi's flashlight dances over the arched ceiling and walls of the lower basilica. As he searches for the door that will lead him to his treasure, his light passes over the images that adorn the walls – they're of angels, saints, apostles, and, yes, of Jesus. He can feel them watching him!

"Oh, forgive me, you Holy Ones," he prays out loud. "If you knew how desperate I am for something of value, you would not condemn me."

Just as he is about to enter the room where his treasure awaits him, his light strikes a painting with images of grotesque-looking people being pulled down to hell. "Oh, *Dio mio*, please do not send me to hell for this. I do love You, dear Lord, but this is for my daughter," he pleads, in the empty, almost tomb-like basilica.

Luigi moves quickly now to get away from the images and his thoughts. "Got to do it now," he reminds himself.

Through the door to the right of the main altar and down a few more stone steps he hastens. There is no light at all in the room, except for the light from his flashlight.

Across the way he sees his treasure. "Oh, this has to be of very great value. It is so beautiful," Luigi continues to talk to himself. It is as if he has to provide an excuse for his actions.

His light strikes a painting with images of grotesque-looking people being pulled down to hell.

The object in the glass case gleams of bright polished silver and nearly shimmers under the beam of his flashlight. In the center of the stand is a piece of paper that is yellowed from age. "Now!" he commands himself.

The light dashes and crashes around the room as Luigi uses the handle of the flashlight to smash the glass protecting the bright ornate silver stand. He grabs the stand and examines it before shoving it into the rucksack. It is heavier than he anticipated and therefore probably even more valuable than the thought. He stares at the yellow paper framed in the center of the stand. Luigi never learned to read, so he has no idea what is written on the paper. "This cannot be very important. Look how yellow it is," he says to himself. He shrugs his shoulders and tosses the paper into his rucksack along with the silver stand. Little does Luigi know that the paper is worth a million times more than the silver stand.

Luigi hurries back into the main part of the lower basilica, stumbling up the low, flat steps. It is pitch dark except for the light from his flashlight. He squeezes back between another set of wooden choir chairs. Now all he has to do is wait here until the guards open the basilica in the morning. In his clever plan, he has decided to pretend to be one of the cleaning people, and just walk out of the basilica with his bag under his arm.

Bored and curious, Luigi decides to take a better look at his treasure. He pulls the stand from the rucksack and uses the light of the flashlight to inspect it. Satisfied with his choice of treasure, he polishes it with the cuff of his shirt. Before placing the silver stand back in the rucksack, Luigi shakes the crumbs out of the bag. Oops! Maybe he isn't such a cautious thief after all! Unnoticed by Luigi, the little yellowed paper that was in the silver stand falls to the floor with the crumbs.

A mournful yet distant cry of a wolf again breaks the silence inside the basilica. Luigi hears it, listens again but only hears the silence of night. Something that feels like a warm breeze brushes his cheek and then is gone. He tries to sleep, but can't.

Morning finally comes and Luigi walks out of the basilica just as he planned, carrying his rucksack and treasure with him.

THE CALL

*IN ANOTHER PART OF ITALY ON THE MORNING AFTER THE
BREAK-IN AT THE BASILICA OF SAINT FRANCIS IN ASSISI*

"This is my favorite time of day," says Riley as
he, his little sister, Delaney, and his aunt, Sister
Philomena, walk through the vineyards owned by the
Sisters of Saint Francis at their convent in Grottaferrata
in Italy. Grottaferrata is a small village that sits high on
the hills above Rome. From the vantage point of the
convent, you can see all of Rome off in the distance.
Between Rome and the convent are several villages
ringed with trees and lakes. It is a very beautiful scene.

Riley and Delaney have been staying with Sister
Philomena at the convent ever since their parents left
them there earlier this summer. Their mom and dad
had business to conduct in southern France and
northern Italy. Their parents are leaders in the
agricultural community in the U.S.A. They travel
around the world to attend conferences and consult
with farming specialists in other countries.

Rather than leaving the children at home with a
nanny, they decided it would be good for them to visit
Sister Philomena, their mother's sister. Surely they
could benefit from living awhile in Italy and learning
about the culture.

At first Sister Philomena was terrified at the thought of caring for children. After all, she is a nun living in a convent – what does she know about children? But it was impossible for her to say "no" to her favorite sister – besides, she truly cherishes her niece and nephew.

Riley just knew this was going to be a dreadful summer. A boy, or young man as he likes to think of himself nowadays, does not belong in a convent with his kid sister and a bunch of nuns. What do nuns do besides go to church and pray?

But things are a lot different than he had expected. The nuns are very nice to him and Delaney. In fact they seem happy to have kids around. And, except for his aunt, these sisters are like farmers. They grow grapes and make wine that is used for Mass at the Vatican and in most of the churches in Rome. They also maintain groves of olive trees that are a source of eating olives as well as olive oil. The few farm animals, cows, goats, and chickens, provide milk, cheese, and eggs for their table. They even have a garden where they grow most of their own vegetables.

But his and Delaney's aunt, Sister Philomena, has a secret that until now has never been shared with her family or anyone outside the convent and Italian law enforcement. In addition to being a nun, Sister Philomena is actually a special investigative agent for the Pope. That's right, the Pope who is head of the entire Catholic Church. As the Pope's special secret agent, Sister Philomena is called upon to help his staff of Swiss Guards and the Italian police investigate and solve crimes related to Church property and business.

Early each morning Riley and Delaney join several of the sisters from the convent to "walk the grapes." This means they stroll through the grape arbors looking for bugs or black spots that may be a sign of fungus. They also pull from the soil any weeds that popped up overnight.

Riley dreams of being a farmer when he grows up. One day he hopes to have acres and acres of grape arbors on a farm back in the U.S.A.

"Do you think grapes will grow in Illinois?" he asks Sister Philomena. "The farmers there mostly grow corn and soybeans. But I want to grow grapes and make wine for the local churches!"

"Maybe you can try a small grape arbor when you go home, just to test the idea. I am sure your father will be happy to help you," suggests Sister Philomena.

Just then Sister Philomena's cell phone rings. Riley is amused that a nun carries a cell phone in the pocket of her habit.

"*Pronto*," Sister answers, as she absentmindedly

Delaney peeks under the leaf to be sure the bug isn't harmed.

picks a little bug from the underside of a grape leaf. Examining it, she decides it's harmless to the grapes and puts the bug back on the leaf. Delaney peeks under the leaf to be sure the bug isn't harmed.

"*Si, si*, Holy Father," Sister Philomena talks excitedly in Italian. She listens intently. "*Grazie.* I will leave immediately."

As she closes the cell phone, she looks at Delaney and Riley. "Now, what do I do with you?!"

The Holy Father, the Pope, has called her to assist in an investigation of a crime at the Basilica of Saint Francis in Assisi, one to two hours northeast of the convent by train. She cannot leave these two children here by themselves, the Reverend Mother has made this very clear! What choice does she have but to take them with her?

"Children, hurry, we need to pack a few things for an overnight stay. We have to go to Assisi right away. The Holy Father has requested my assistance to investigate a crime."

Riley and Delaney have met the Pope on several occasions. In fact, they have even eaten pizza with him in his apartment in the Vatican. That was after they got lost in Saint Peter's tomb on their very first day in Italy. What an adventure that was!

Now Riley's heart races as he realizes there is yet another adventure awaiting them!

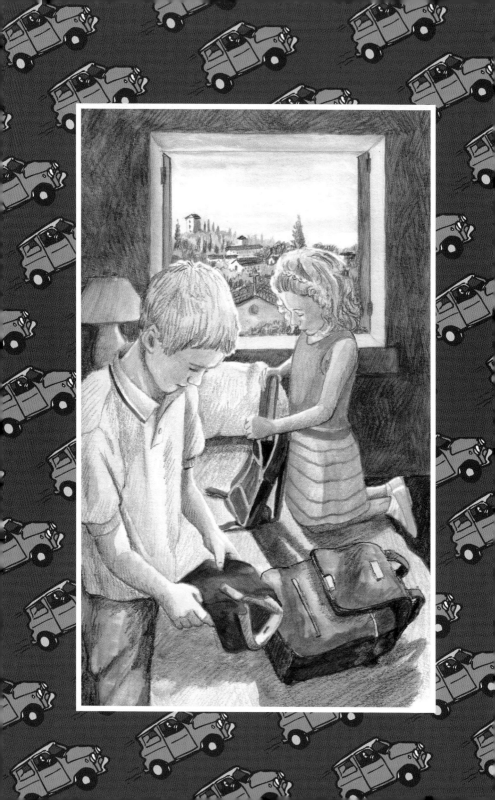

TRAIN TO ASSISI

"*Rapidamente!* Quickly, Riley and Delaney!
There is no time to delay. Please put your pajamas, a
clean change of underwear, and a change of clothes in
your backpacks. Oh, and put in your toothbrushes,
something small to play with, and a book to read,"
says Sister Philomena, remembering that somehow
the children have to be kept busy. She paces back and
forth talking to herself in Italian.

She looks at the children and they look back at
her, as if to say, "What's all the fuss, and where are
we going?"

Sister Philomena explains, "the reason the Pope
is sending me (well, actually us) to Assisi, is because
there was a break-in at the Basilica of Saint Francis
either last night or early this morning. Someone stole
the Chartula of Saint Francis. The Chartula is just a
small piece of paper, but it contains the Blessing for
Brother Leo and the Prayer of Praises written by Saint
Francis – in his own handwriting! It's irreplaceable
and priceless. The Holy Father is praying that we find it.

"The Chartula was in a specially designed silver stand inside a specially designed display case inside the relic room inside the basilica. The display case was smashed and the silver stand with the Chartula inside was stolen. Pray to God that we find it!"

As soon as Delaney and Riley have their bags ready, Sister grabs the black valise she keeps packed for these special Papal investigative assignments.

"Is the Pope sending a car for us?" asks a hopeful Riley. Riley likes the idea of being driven around in the Pope's car. It makes him feel very important.

"Not this time. We're taking the train. It's faster. Sister Lisa Renee will drive us to the station," says a breathless Sister Philomena.

Outside the iron gates that are the front door of the convent, and in front of the big statue of Saint Francis, Sister Lisa Renee is waiting in a little red car. The car's fenders and bumpers are dented and the paint is dull.

"Is that car safe?" Riley gasps.

"Andiamo! Andiamo!" pleads Sister Lisa Renee in Italian. She is waving her arms inside the car like a crazy woman.

By now Riley knows that *andiamo* means "let's

go or hurry up" in Italian. Their aunt uses the word a
lot when she wants to get them moving.

Riley grabs Delaney and pulls her into the
backseat of the little car. They have to sit on their
backpacks to see out the dirty windows, because the
springs in the backseat are broken.

Sister Lisa Renee forces the car into gear, pops the
clutch, and guns the engine. The car leaps forward.
Stops. Leaps forward again. Stops. Chugs a few
times. Finally it rolls forward and accelerates. Riley
and Delaney tumble around in the
backseat like bouncing Ping-Pong
balls.

"Sister, you are going to give us
all whiplash," chuckles Sister
Philomena. "We do need to get to
the train station in one piece."

"Mi dispiace," says Sister Lisa
Renee, then rattles on

The three rush to board the train just as it begins to leave the station.

in Italian, waving one hand then another above the steering wheel.

Riley knows that *mi dispiace* means "I'm sorry," but the rest is lost in translation. It sounds like Sister Lisa Renee is scolding the car, telling it to cooperate, but he isn't sure.

The car comes to an abrupt stop at the train station, just missing the barricade that keeps cars away from the building. Now Riley knows how all those dents got in the car.

The three rush to board the train just as it begins to leave the station. Stumbling down the aisle of the moving train, Riley and Delaney flop into two big blue, side-by-side seats. Sister Philomena sits across the aisle from them. The train has huge windows that allow the passengers to have full view of the city and the countryside. Riley expected the train to be dirty and full of beggars and poor people. But this train is very clean and very nice. Many men riding the train are dressed in business suits. Some tourists are happily checking maps as they look out the windows and gesture to each other.

"I'm hungry," says Delaney, who has been unusually quiet today. Some days she doesn't stop talking; other days you would not know she's around because she is so quiet. So far today has been a quiet day and Sister Philomena hopes it will stay that way.

Realizing that they are about to miss their noon meal, Sister Philomena says, "Well then, shall we all go to the dining car for a little lunch? We don't arrive in Assisi for another hour."

Sitting in the dining car they enjoy a nice lunch of *zuppa* (that means soup in Italian), lasagna, cookies, and *latte* or milk for the children and an espresso coffee for Sister Philomena. As they eat they watch the countryside pass by. Sister helps them with the Italian names of the things they see. They pass through *vigneti* (vineyards), groves of *olivo* (olive trees), pastures where *pecora* (sheep) graze, and *città* (towns).

"I see a *pastore*, a shepherd," shouts Delaney, pointing to a man standing in the middle of a herd of sheep. "A *mucca!*" she shouts seeing a cow next to the train tracks. Although Delaney is too young to read difficult words, she is learning to speak Italian easily.

"Assisi, next stop!" shouts the conductor as he passes through the train.

Sister Philomena points out the window to the right. "That's Assisi up on the hill. That's where we are going."

"Is that a real place?" questions Riley, seeing the hill town of Umbria for the first time. "It looks like a postcard – like it's painted on the side of that hill!"

"Is that a real place?" questions Riley.

The end of town nearest them has a long building reaching out and down the hillside. The building looks like a slice of honeycomb. Sitting on top of the long honeycomb-like building is big church with a cross on top.

"That's the Basilica di San Francesco, the Church of Saint Francis of Assisi," explains Sister Philomena. "It is one of the most famous and beautiful basilicas in all the world. It's also the scene of the crime we have come to investigate."

"Can we help you with the investigation?" asks Riley. His stomach is filled to the brim with butterflies as he anticipates being in this new place and helping his aunt solve the crime. "Delaney and I can look for clues, if that's OK with you."

"What would help me the most would be for you two to remain out of the way and be quiet," Sister Philomena tells them.

Seeing the disappointment on both Riley's and Delaney's face, she changes her mind. "Sure, you can look for clues. Keep your eyes and ears open, then later today you can tell me about everything you find!"

"*Andiamo*, children. The train stops only for a minute and we have to hop off quickly."

A police car with its blue and white lights flashing is parked at the front of the train station. "Uh, oh! Has there been a crime here in the train station?"

"No, silly boy," says Sister Philomena. "That's our ride."

Seeing Delaney headed in the opposite direction, Sister calls out, *"Venuto qui, venuto qui.* Come here, come here, Delaney." Sister Philomena grabs Delaney by the hand just before she enters the *Tabacchi* shop with dolls and trinkets in the window. "Come, get in the car."

A serious-looking man in a uniform steps forward, salutes, and extends his hand to Sister Philomena. Riley is impressed with the formality of it all and the courtesy shown to his aunt.

The uniformed man takes their bags and puts them in the trunk of the police car. The children climb into the backseat while Sister Philomena sits up front. The car pulls away from the station with its lights flashing and now with the siren blaring. *Wheee-haaaw. Wheee-haaaw. Whee-haaaw.*

Riley is so excited – he cannot believe this is happening to him. The kids back home will never believe he got to ride in an Italian police car with the siren going.

"When we arrive at the basilica, I will be meeting with the Padre Custode of the basilica, the *polizia* (the civil police who investigate crimes) and the *carabinieri* (army police who maintain order). You may listen and watch what is going on, but promise me you will stay out of the way and not interrupt."

Riley and Delaney look at each other with excited eyes and shake their heads up and down.

"The Padre Custode has closed the basilica until the preliminary investigation is complete. There are thousands of pilgrims waiting to visit the famous and holy basilica and the tomb of Saint Francis," says Sister Philomena. "The investigative team must work very fast."

"What's the Italian word for wolf?" Riley asks his aunt. He just saw a grey wolf standing in the middle of an olive grove along the roadway. The wolf seems to be staring right at him.

"Umm, the Italian word for wolf is *lupo,*" says Sister Philomena. She is deep in thought about the upcoming investigation and doesn't even ask Riley why he wanted to know.

The wolf seems to be staring right at him.

THE BASILICA

The police car with flashing lights and siren blaring, ...*Whee-haaaw, Whee-haaaw*... stops in front of the massive doors of the basilica. Serious-looking men in dark uniforms stand guard. Alongside the uniformed guards are several friars dressed in brown robes with white ropes tied around their waists. They look worried.

Hundreds of tourists crowd around the roped-off entrance. The people stretch and strain to see what is happening. They must wonder why the police officer is taking a nun and two kids into the basilica. The faces in the crowd show a mix of worry, interest, and curiosity.

As they enter the basilica, the children are struck by the coolness of the ancient stone church – a welcome relief from the hot summer sun. It takes a few moments for their eyes to adjust to the darkness. Although the basilica is very large inside and the ceiling is high, Riley and Delaney feel as if they have walked into a dark cave.

In front of them is an altar. Signs in Italian and English say "This area reserved for Mass and prayers." Sister Philomena makes a quick genuflection and Sign of the Cross; the kids do the same. There is no one else around. The entire basilica appears empty except for them and their police escort.

Riley and Delaney are filled with wonder as they turn into the main part of the basilica. A huge arched ceiling covers the entire length of a long main aisle. The ceiling is dark blue and dotted with gold stars that seem to flicker. It's like they're walking under a starry blue sky. It is awesome.

Riley and Delaney notice several small chapels opening off the long main aisle. These chapels are filled with flowers, paintings, statues, and candles.

At the end of the long main aisle is a big high altar. Hanging directly above the altar is a painted crucifix. It looks like it's suspended in midair. The ceiling above the crucifix is divided into four parts, and each part is filled with painted pictures.

"Look, there are paintings on the walls and ceilings, just like at the Pope's house," observes an excited Delaney. She has been scolded several times for drawing on the walls at home, and more recently, in the convent. She wonders why is it permitted here and in the Pope's house, but when she draws on the wall, they tell her she is a naughty girl.

"Oh my, yes," says Sister Philomena as they approach the high altar. "Famous artists like Giotto working hundreds of years ago painted the inside of this basilica. These paintings tell of the lives of Jesus and of Saint Francis. Other paintings in the basilica tell stories from the Bible and about other saints' lives. There are even larger pictures on the walls upstairs, in what is called the upper basilica.

"But how come they put pictures all over the walls?" questions Delaney.

"It was a way of spreading the faith," explains Sister Philomena. "Back then people didn't have very many books. In fact, a lot of people couldn't even read. But people did go to church. The artists painted on the walls and ceilings of churches so that even if people did not have books or could not read, they would still be able to know the stories of Jesus, the Bible, and the saints through pictures."

Voices are heard coming from a doorway just beyond the high altar. Sister Philomena and the children follow the sound. They descend the few low stone steps that form the entrance into the large room. Riley gets goose bumps as he realizes he is entering a real crime scene. This is the kind of stuff he has read about in books, but only dreamed of ever being a part

of. Now here he is, about to help his aunt investigate
a crime. He can feel this turning into another very
great adventure.

Several investigators, some in uniforms and
some in street clothes, are in the room. They are
examining a shattered display case and trying not to
step on the glass that is all over the floor.

As Sister Philomena and the children enter the
room, called a reliquary or relic room, the men turn
and half-bow to Sister Philomena. Riley is amazed
and thrilled to see the respect shown his aunt. They
clearly have been waiting for her to take charge of the
investigation. His mom would never believe this.
She has always said that her sister, their aunt, was a
scatterbrain. Wow, was she wrong.

Sister Philomena immediately opens the black
valise she brought with her from Grottaferrata. The
kids crowd in close to her to get a glimpse of what's
inside the mysterious black bag. First she pulls out a
roll of yellow tape. She hands it to an investigator and
he uses the tape to seal off the crime scene. Next she
takes out a notebook and pencil and begins to ask
questions. Every so often she'll make a note in her
book and ask one of the investigators to do something.
Riley tries to figure out what they are saying to each
other, but they are speaking in Italian and he just
doesn't understand the language well enough, yet.

In no time Sister Philomena has all the investigators busy doing something. Some are dusting for fingerprints. Others are picking up small pieces of glass and itsy-bitsy fibers and putting them in plastic bags. Two investigators are on their cell phones.

After a while Sister Philomena glances in the direction of the children. They have been so quiet she almost forgot they were in the room. Riley has been watching the investigation with great interest. He wonders what kind of clues he can uncover. It looks a little more complicated than he thought. Delaney is fussing with a scarf that she has taken out of her backpack.

"What's that?" asks Sister Philomena.

"It's my wings. Look, I'm an angel," says Delaney, pulling the scarf over the back of her arms and flapping her elbows like wings. "You said I could bring a toy. This is what I brought!"

Quite clever, thinks Sister Philomena. Kids are really amazing.

"Why don't you children go and look around the basilica while it's closed to other visitors. See how many angel pictures you can find, Delaney. Later you can both describe to me what you found. But do not touch anything – just look! And do not open any closed doors. *Capite?* Understand?"

Riley and Delaney turn and race each other up the low-rising stone steps. Delaney's scarf is now flung over her shoulders and flows like a cape.

"That's a picture of Jesus on the Cross," says Riley as he and his sister re-enter the basilica and face a painted wall. "Delaney, see the figures with halos around their heads. Those are pictures of saints. The ones with wings are angels. I learned that in my religion class."

"I'm an angel too," says Delaney, as she transforms her scarf back into wings.

"That picture there looks like Mary holding the baby Jesus with Joseph standing right behind them. It must be a nativity scene. These are the Three Wise Men," Riley says pointing to the figures in the painting

that appear to be bringing presents to the infant Jesus.
Delaney tilts her head to try and figure it out.

"Those pictures up there make me dizzy," says
Delaney, turning in circles as she looks up at the ceiling
over the high altar. Of the four sets of paintings,
Delaney decides she likes the one called *Obedience* the
best. "Look, that one shows a lady with her finger to
her lips. She is saying 'shush – be quiet.' Think she is
reminding us to be good? Hey, she's got wings. She's
an angel, just like me!"

"Let's go down there," suggests Delaney,
pointing to a dimly lit open stairwell.

Riley reaches out and takes Delaney's hand.
As they start to go down the stairs he gets that feeling
you get when something important is about to
happen – or something scary is going to happen –
or both.

At the bottom of the stairs they enter into a
shadowy room. Facing them is a chiseled stone tower.
It's about ten feet wide and twenty or more feet tall.
Metal bars surround it. In front of the stone is an altar
with burning candles and white flowers. The candles
and flowers go all the way around the stone tower.
Riley and Delaney quietly, cautiously inch their way
around the huge stone.

Just on the other side Riley finds a poster with
information written in several languages. He reads
the one in English and explains it to Delaney. "The
sign says that Saint Francis is buried here – it's his
tomb."

Delaney sucks in a gulp of air. She's learned
that there are a lot of tombs in Italy, and tombs are
places where you visit dead people.

"Listen to this," says Riley, grabbing his little
sister to keep her from running away. "The stone and
iron gates were designed to protect the body of Saint
Francis. Hundreds of years ago thieves would steal
the saints' bones and clothes and stuff and sell them
as relics. Because the friars didn't want thieves to
bother Francis's body, they built this huge strong wall
around him."

"So, OK. Let's go tell Aunt Philomena what we
found," demands Delaney. She is scared and wants
out of this strange dark place.

"We can go. But let's first say a prayer to Saint
Francis to ask him to ask God to protect us and to
help Sister Philomena find the stolen Chartula," says
Riley. He drags his sister to the front of the altar
before the tomb of Saint Francis. They kneel and
say the *Our Father* together. After a quick *Sign of the
Cross*, Delaney stands up, turns and runs back up
the stairs.

As they start to go down the stairs he gets that feeling you get when something important is about to happen...

He nearly scares her to death.

Sister Philomena is still busy with the investigation. Wisely, the children decide not to interrupt her.

"Let's play hide-and-seek," says Delaney. "This place is perfect, even if it is pretty scary. But no fair going back to the tomb!"

"You go first – go hide," says Riley, covering his eyes and counting to ten.

"Here I come, ready or not."

Turning around, he spots his little sister in a dark corner not too far away. She is curled up behind some big brown chairs, but her scarf is sticking out. He tiptoes over to where she is hiding.

"Boo!"

He nearly scares her to death.

As she jumps, Delaney kicks a piece of paper from beneath the dark wooden chair. She picks it up and examines it. "This looks really old," she says, handing it to Riley. "I think it's been here hundreds of years, just like everything else."

"Could be," says Riley. "It's faded, but I think the writing is in Italian or Latin. There are words on both sides."

"Holy smoke!" he shouts. "I think this is it – the Chartula! Let's show it to Aunt Philomena."

Delaney grabs the piece of paper and takes off running. "I saw it first. I get to show her!" Riley chases after her.

"Aunt Philomena, look what we've found!" shouts Delaney, as she bursts into the quiet room, wildly waving the piece of paper above her head like a small flag.

At first Sister Philomena wants to ignore the interruption. However, all the other investigators look up, so Sister realizes she has to attend to the child. "What is it, Delaney? I asked you not to touch anything," she reminds the little girl.

Taking the piece of paper, Sister blurts out, "*Oh, Dio mio! Oh, Dio mio!* It's the Chartula!" She makes the *Sign of the Cross* and looks up as tears flood her eyes.

The other investigators look on in amazement as Sister gently holds the fragile and precious paper in her trembling hands.

Just then Riley thinks he hears a wolf howling off in the distance. He touches his cheek as a warm breeze passes over it. Then it's gone.

"Aunt Philomena, look what we've found!"

THE CHARTULA

"Is that really it?" questions Riley. "Delaney just kicked it out from under one of those big old wooden chairs out there."

"Oh, my heavens! Thank you, Lord! Thank you, Delaney! Thank you, Riley! God bless you!" Sister Philomena grabs the children, giving them hugs and kisses. "Children, this is the Chartula, the precious piece of paper that was stolen last night in the break-in. It's the one we have been looking for – the major focus for this entire investigation."

"This paper and the prayers on it are from the hand of Saint Francis. Look, on one side is written a *Blessing for Brother Leo* and the other side has *The Praises of God*. Saint Francis wrote these prayers in the year 1225 and gave them to his best friend, Brother Leo. Brother Leo kept the paper folded and close to his heart until the day he died. This piece of paper is considered one of the most precious relics from the life of Saint Francis of Assisi. It was stolen last night. Now it's found! Praise the Lord!"

Laying the precious paper onto a piece of fine

linen to preserve it until it can be safely returned to the display case, Sister Philomena says, "Wait a minute children, let me read to you the prayers written by Saint Francis. We'll make it our prayer of thanksgiving."

As she begins to read, Riley remembers the prayers he and Delaney said before the tomb of Saint Francis. Those prayers are being answered! All the investigators stop to listen as Sister Philomena reads the prayers printed on the very old paper.

Blessing for Brother Leo

May the Lord bless you and keep you.
May He show his face to you
And be merciful to you.
May He turn his countenance
To you and give you peace.

B. Leo **T**

The Lord Bless You

"See that sort of 'T' there on the paper? That is how Saint Francis signed his name. It's called a 'tau' and it was his style for the Cross.

Then Sister Philomena turns the paper over
and reads:

The Praises of God

You are the holy Lord God Who does wonderful things!
You are strong. You are Great. You are the most high.
You are the almighty king. You holy Father,
King of heaven and earth.

You are three and one, the Lord God of gods;
You are the good, all good, the highest good,
Lord God Living and true.

You are love, charity; You are wisdom, You are humility.
You are patience, You are beauty, You are meekness,
You are security, You are rest,
You are gladness and joy, You are our hope, You are justice,
You are moderation, You are all our riches to sufficiency.

You are beauty, You are meekness
You are the protector, You are our custodian and defender,
You are strength, You are refreshment. You are our hope,
You are our faith, You are our charity,
You are all our sweetness, You are our eternal life;
Great and wonderful Lord, Almighty God, Merciful Savior.

"So we found a pretty important clue?" asks
Riley. He is overcome with that sense you get when
you've done something really good, so good that you
don't believe it's you that did it.

"Indeed you have! It doesn't solve the mystery,
but it does tell us something about the crime.

"This paper was inside a silver stand, that was
inside that specially designed display case. Last night
someone smashed the case and took out the stand and
the Chartula. For some reason, the Chartula is no
longer with the silver holder.

"Show us where you found the paper – perhaps
the silver stand is nearby," suggests one of the
investigators.

The men follow the children to the choir stalls
while Sister Philomena places the Chartula carefully
between two pieces of linen and then secures it in her
black valise.

The investigators seal off, then search the area
where Delaney and Riley found the paper. There is
no silver stand to be found. However, in their search
they do find a few breadcrumbs and a straw that
smells like it had wine on it. The crumbs and straw,
along with the other evidence taken from the relic
room, will be sent to the Italian Crime Laboratory in
Milan for further examination.

The crime team finally is able to take a break.

Although they feel compelled now to open the basilica to visitors and pilgrims, this area around the wooden choir stalls and the relic room must remain off-limits until the investigation is finished.

"Why would someone be so dumb as to take the silver stand and leave the precious paper?" asks one of the investigators.

"Well, if I were a thief," says Riley, "I would much prefer silver over paper. I could sell the silver, but what could I do with an old piece of paper? Especially if I did not know it had value."

"Very wise deduction," comments the investigator. "Perhaps the thief cannot read. Or, maybe he is ignorant of the value of the Chartula. You're pretty smart – just like that aunt of yours."

Sister Philomena is so very proud of her niece and nephew. If it were not for their playing hide-and-seek in the basilica, they might never have found the precious paper, the Chartula. In fact, it probably would have been swept out with the trash. A chill runs down her spine.

But she realizes this crime investigation is not yet over. They still need to recover the silver stand and to catch the thief.

SAINT FRANCIS

Sister Philomena decides the other investigators can carry on while she and the children take a break. The Saint Francis Guest House where they will be staying overnight is on the other side of Assisi from the Basilica di San Francesco. A walk through town will calm her nerves and may relax the children. They are certainly on a high after finding the Chartula.

"Come this way. Let me show you the other parts of the basilica," says Sister Philomena. She leads the children halfway up a steep stone stairway that opens into the second story of a courtyard. Several friars dressed in their brown robes and rope belts are busy in the courtyard. Some are working in the garden, others are reading books, and one has his arms outstretched and is looking up to the sky.

"Why do they dress like that?" questions Riley.

"Their way of dress is reminiscent of the simple tunic that Saint Francis and the other Friars Minor wore in the 1200s. The friars have taken vows of poverty and have no need for fancy dress. Like many religious sisters, the friars neither want nor need much more than a simple habit. Their belts, like mine, have three knots. See," she says as she holds out the rope belt to her habit. "The three knots represent the vows we take – that of poverty, obedience, and chastity."

"What's up there?" asks Riley, turning and looking up the next flight of steep stone steps.

"That's the church on top of the honeycomb-like buildings that we saw from the train. It's called the upper basilica. The place we just came from, where you found the Chartula, is called the lower basilica. Come, let's take a look."

The upper basilica looms over them like a giant. They climb the rest of the way up the steep stone stairway and enter the upper basilica. Light streams through the high-up windows. Whereas in the lower basilica they felt like they were entering a cave, this

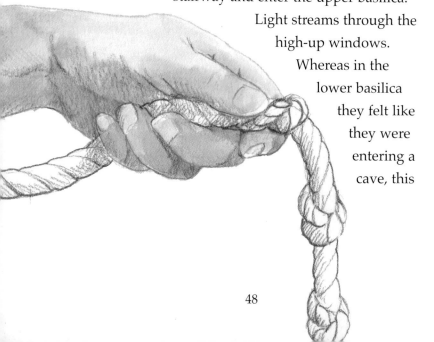

area feels like walking into a ray of sunshine.

"Look, more places to hide," says Delaney. Wooden choir stalls, dark and ornate like the ones downstairs where they found the precious paper, are set against the back wall of the upper basilica. Little do they realize that this was the first hideout for the still unidentified thief.

On the wall facing them is another picture of the crucified Christ. Sister Philomena has the children study the picture and tell her what they see.

"Lots of angels!" claims Delaney. "The sky and trees are full of them."

"Did someone try to scrape the paint off the walls?" asks Riley. Some of the pictures look like they have parts missing.

"No, Riley. I am afraid some of the paintings have faded over time. Also, a few years ago earthquakes shook the walls so hard that some of the walls and the pictures painted on them just crumbled," Sister Philomena explains. "Padre Custode is working very had to get them all restored."

"Pictures painted directly onto the plaster walls like these are called frescoes. See how the light from the big windows brings out the colors in the frescoes.

"So how come Saint Francis got to be so important?" questions Riley.

"Saint Francis was really called upon by God to do His work on earth. In fact, Francis is probably responsible for bringing more people to Christ than any other human person. Let's look at some of these paintings. They can tell us a lot about his life – I can fill in the blanks as we walk," says Sister Philomena.

"Saint Francis was born here in Assisi around the year 1182. That was a time long before there were cars or trains or anything of that nature. Francis was the son of a very successful merchant named Pietro Bernadone. Because the family Bernadone was very wealthy, Francis was given the nicest things in life and never had to worry about anything. Kind of like you kids," she teases.

"Well, Francis led what I would call a 'fast life.' He and his friends were high-spirited, well-dressed, jovial, and tried to outdo one another in foolishness.

"Mr. Bernadone, Francis's father, wanted him to be a shop owner and take over the family business. For a while, Francis went along with this plan, and he was a great salesman.

"However, Francis had other ideas. He wanted to be a warrior, and so he joined forces in a local war against the people of nearby Perugia. Not long after he took up arms, Francis was captured and thrown into jail, where he stayed for over a year. It was during this time in jail that he started to think differently.

"After he got out of jail he felt confused but he still had a desire to be a warrior. That's when Francis decided to become a knight and fight in the Crusades. The Crusades were a series of wars fought to defend Christianity and save the Christian sites in the Holy Land from destruction by the Turks or Muslims. In order to fight in the Crusades, men had to be knighted by the Pope.

"On his journey to Rome to see the Pope and to be made a knight, Francis began to see all the beautiful things around him and he began to think more about God. He began to pray and to listen to what God wanted him to do with his life. Much to the dismay of his father, Francis turned around and came home. He never made it to Rome and never joined the Crusades.

"One day, while Francis was praying before the crucifix in the little church of San Damiano he heard Jesus speak to him from the cross. Jesus said, 'Go, Francis, and rebuild my church.'

"Look here, this fresco shows Francis in prayer before the crucifix at San Damiano.

"At first Francis thought God wanted him to fix

"It was during this time in jail that he started to think differently."

up the little church at San Damiano. He did that. Then he went and fixed the broken-down Church of the Blessed Virgin in the nearby woods of the Portiuncola. As he worked, Francis studied the Bible. He was especially impressed by the passage in the Gospel of Matthew, Chapter 10, where Jesus told His Apostles to go out and preach and heal the lost souls. The Apostles were to do so without pay, because they received their faith at no cost. And they weren't to take any gold or silver, no sack for the journey, no second tunic or sandals, or walking stick. They just had to trust in God to provide for their needs.

"Well, it wasn't long before Francis started giving away all that he owned, and some of his father's possessions too. He gave them to the poor and to the lepers. This made his father furious! Mr. Bernadone demanded that Francis give back everything and repay him for all the money his son had given to the poor. His father even called the bishop to come and talk some sense into Francis. When confronted, Francis stripped himself naked in the middle of town, gave his clothes back to his father, and went off with nothing. This picture shows that," says Sister Philomena, pointing to another fresco.

"I bet that's the bishop holding a towel around Saint Francis," observes Riley. "Saint Francis already has a saint's halo around his head. That's cool."

"Very observant Riley," says Sister Philomena.

"Dressed in a simple tunic, he traveled through the area telling people about Jesus Christ and reading to them from the Bible. Soon several other men joined him. One of them was Brother Leo, the one to whom the prayer was written on that little piece of paper you found in the basilica, the Chartula that the thief threw away.

"Anyway, all the men who joined up with Francis were called the Friars Minor. They owned absolutely nothing and existed solely on the donations from others. But, oh, did they change hearts and bring people to the Lord. It was the Church with a capital 'C', the whole Catholic Church, that Jesus wanted him to fix!

"The time came when the friars wanted to become an order of brothers recognized by the Catholic Church. Francis, Leo and some other friars went to Rome to ask for the Pope's permission. This is shown in the next fresco. It took some doing, but the Pope finally gave approval. Today there are hundreds of different Orders of Saint Francis. There are priests, brothers, sisters, and even lay people. In my convent in Grottaferratta, we are an Order of Saint Francis."

"Dressed in a simple tunic, he traveled through the area telling people about Jesus Christ and reading to them from the Bible."

"Saint Francis saw the face of God in everything, but especially in nature."

"That is a very famous fresco there by the exit door," explains Sister Philomena as they approach the last of the pictures. "It is the one of Saint Francis preaching to the birds. See how the birds seem to be listening and not flying away. Saint Francis saw the face of God in everything, but especially in nature. He taught that everything we have and see and breathe is a gift from God.

"Let me tell you one more story about Saint Francis. He is well known for being able to talk to animals. One day Saint Francis was called upon to solve a problem with a wolf in the nearby town of Gubbio. The people of Gubbio were up in arms. A wolf had been killing and eating their chickens and other small animals. They were afraid the wolf would snatch and eat one their children. The only solution the people of Gubbio knew of was to kill the wolf. They wanted Francis to help them.

"Francis, however, had another idea. Saint Francis believed the wolf had as much right to live in the area as did the people. Cautiously, Francis approached the wolf. The wolf looked mean and hungry. Francis explained to the wolf that the people of Gubbio were angry and that they wanted to kill him. Then Francis struck a deal. Francis promised the wolf that the people of Gubbio would feed him if he would just stop stealing their animals. The wolf agreed! He even offered his paw to Saint Francis to seal the agreement. The people of Gubbio were thankful and cooperated by putting out food for the wolf. After that the townspeople and the wolf all lived happily ever after."

"Are there any wolves where we are going to stay tonight?" asks a very concerned Delaney. She now has her scarf wrapped around her like a mummy.

"No, funny girl," says Sister Philomena reassuringly. "Assisi is much too busy for the wolves today."

"But I saw a wolf when we left the train station this morning," says Riley. "It was a big gray wolf with bright scary-looking eyes. You told me the Italian word for wolf was *lupo*. Do you remember?"

"I do remember you asking," says Sister Philomena. "Perhaps it was a big dog you saw. It would be very rare to see a wolf in these parts today."

"The wolf even offered his paw to Saint Francis to seal the agreement."

BEGGAR MAN

V ia San Francesco is the main street leading away from the basilica towards the center of town and the main piazza. The street is narrow, crowded with people, and flanked by shops on each side.

"How come there are so many people here and how come there are so many shops selling statues of the same guy?" asks Riley.

"Lots of tourists and pilgrims come to Assisi because it is a Holy Place," explains Sister Philomena. "Many of the people who lived here in the 1200s became saints. They worked very hard to spread the word of God throughout the region.

"The shops?" continues Sister Philomena. "People like to take home a small remembrance of this place. The 'guy' you refer to in all those statues is Saint Francis. Look in this window. See all the statues of Saint Francis with a bird on his shoulder and a wolf beside him – they are supposed to remind you of the stories of the Gubbio wolf and how Francis would talk to the birds."

"Sure," says Riley. You could almost see the light bulb going off in his head. "The statue in front of your convent. It's a statue of Saint Francis with the wolf and birds. It looks just like the ones in the shop windows, only a lot bigger. It's the Gubbio wolf, isn't it?"

"One and the same," says Sister Philomena, proud that her nephew made the connection.

Just now Riley feels something stirring in his inner being. A thought crosses his mind that there may be some connection between the Gubbio wolf, the wolf he saw this morning, and the break-in at the basilica. Something's there but he just cannot put his finger on it. This will take some more thinking. He decides not to say anything more to Sister Philomena – she already believes he is imagining the wolf, the *lupo*.

They continue walking along the now very narrow streets, where the doorways open right onto the roadway. When cars come by, everyone has to step aside and into doorways to avoid being hit. Some side streets are actually made of steps going up or down. There are pots of flowers everywhere and people's laundry is hung high above the streets.

"Run ahead and scout it out. Be little investigators and tell me everything you see," Sister Philomena says to the children. "But if you come to a fork in the road, either wait there for me to catch up to you or come back

to me. I don't want you getting lost. Assisi streets are full of angles, twists and turns."

"I see another church," says Riley, looking over the top of a wall and down at the small church of Saint Peter. "And there's another! I can see a shiny dome on a big church in the middle of that little town," he says pointing way out over the wall to the plain below and the small town of Santa Maria degli Angeli.

"There are a lot of churches in and around Assisi," chuckles Sister Philomena. "If we have time, we will visit some of my favorites before we leave."

"Great," says Riley sarcastically, scrunching up his face at the thought of visiting churches.

Sister Philomena just smiles and ignores his comment.

Continuing to look over the wall, Riley is amazed. "It looks like a picture out of a book. I see vineyards and fields . . . hills . . .trees. Look out there, it looks like there's a snake cutting through the valley. Is that our train?"

"Yes it is," says Sister Philomena. They spend a few minutes just gazing at the Umbrian countryside below them.

Rushing back to find her aunt and Riley, Delaney sings out, "I found six cats and a fountain

with water spurting out of animals' mouths."

"Good. Go on ahead and wait for us at the foun-
tain. I know a little shop near there where we can
have a *gelato* before going on to the guest house," says
Sister Philomena. "But leave the cats alone. I think
Assisi must have a thousand cats for every church!
And that makes for a lot of cats."

They walk up the street to the center of town
and the main square, named Piazza del Commune.
The *piazza* looks like a large courtyard surrounded by
shops, a post office, a really old church, and several
restaurants. Most of the restaurants have outside
tables and chairs. The *piazza* is crowded with people –
some are eating, some just seem to be visiting with
friends, two men look to be talking more with their
hands than their mouths, and a group of teenagers go
walking by arm in arm and singing an Italian song.
At the far end of the *piazza* is the huge fountain with
the water-spouting animals that Delaney discovered.
They find a table near the fountain and order their
gelato. *Gelato* is the delicious Italian ice cream that is
made daily with fresh fruit and other ingredients. It is
creamy and tangy and cold and refreshing all at the
same time. Ever since they had it at the Pope's house
earlier this summer, Delaney and Riley have become
big fans of *gelato*.

They find a table near the fountain and order their gelato.

After eating their *gelato*, Sister Philomena, Riley and Delaney walk up a narrow street, Corso Mazzini, to the Sisters of Saint Francis Guest House. On the way, Sister Philomena points out the Basilica di Santa Chiara, or Saint Clare's Basilica. "We will stop there and pay our respects to the sisters in the morning, before going back to the crime scene. The head sister there is one of my dearest friends."

As they pass by, Riley notices a man in shabby green and gray clothes sitting in front of Saint Clare's Basilica. At first Riley thinks the man's a beggar, but the man doesn't have a cup or hat set out for donations. He's just sitting there with a big rucksack beside him, gazing at the basilica. As they walk past the man, he looks up. His eyes meet Riley's eyes. Riley is shaken.

The look of the man's eyes is almost the same look that Riley saw in the eyes of the wolf this morning on the way from the train station. Suddenly a warm breeze fills the air. Then it passes.

Very unusual – very mysterious! Riley suddenly feels afraid. But, rather than say something to his aunt about the man, Riley walks on by. Perhaps he is just imagining things.

Across the street from the Guest House is a park with woods, paths, and an outdoor theater. It is one of the nicer small parks they have found in Italy.

Sister Philomena lets the children go exploring in the woods while she sits quietly and thinks about the crime investigation. She pulls out her little book and reviews her notes:

- Display case smashed
- Contents missing
- Chartula found in children's hiding place!!!!
- Silver stand missing
- Evidence thief spent time there (found crumbs and a straw)
- Must have happened in the middle of the night

"What has happened to the silver stand?" she asks herself. "Who is the thief and why did he or she do it?"

Sister Philomena can hear the children laughing and shouting in the background. The park is a safe place and they are having fun. It's a good time for her to catch up on her prayers. The activities of the day have been so demanding that she feels as if she has gotten behind on this responsibility. She bows her head, closes her eyes, and sinks into deep prayer.

THE WOLF

Riley and Delaney can see Sister Philomena sitting on the park bench with her head down and her eyes closed. They have seen her like this before. It looks like she is sleeping, but Riley knows that she is deep in prayer. It's called contemplative prayer, and she can sit motionless this way for a very long time.

"I'm tired. Let's go sit on the swings," says Delaney.

They sit and swing for a while. From the playground they can see the road that goes between the park and the Guest House where they are staying. The park is on a hill so they can also see the olive groves and farmhouses on the hillside below. There are several footpaths worn bare from people walking up and down the hills.

All of a sudden a big gray wolf appears before them. It's just on the other side of the road. The wolf and Riley make eye contact. The wolf turns and begins to walk down the hill. He stops, looks back at Riley,

then circles around and heads back down the hill.

"Delaney, do you see the wolf?" asks Riley. He wants to be sure it isn't his imagination.

"Yes, it looks like a big silver dog," says Delaney.

"What's he doing? Do we need to be afraid of him? Maybe I should get Aunt Philomena."

"No, don't bother her. I think the wolf wants us to follow him," says Riley. "See how he keeps going in circles and then looking back at me? He's saying 'follow me.'"

"But where's he going?" asks Delaney. "I don't want to get lost."

"Come on, we won't get lost," says Riley. "Aunt Philomena won't even know we're gone. If the wolf leads us away from the footpath, we can just turn around and run back to the park."

After looking in both directions, Riley and Delaney cross the road in front of the park. The wolf marches off a safe distance in front of them and they follow. The wolf leads them down the hill through the olive groves and pastures. Riley cannot help but think of Saint Francis and the other friars. They probably walked down this hill a million times – just like this. Francis wasn't afraid of the Gubbio wolf, and they don't need to be afraid of this wolf.

Soon they come upon a small stone church. This

Soon they come upon a small stone church.

church looks like it's a million years old and seems like it's in the middle of nowhere. The wolf lets out a howl and circles around in front of the church – then it just disappears.

"How weird," observes Riley. "Now what? I bet the wolf was telling us to go into the church. What do you think?" he asks his sister.

By now Delaney is wrapped up in the scarf that she brought with her from Grottaferrata. But rather than wings, it is now a shawl used to stave off the chill of the goose bumps she's feeling. "I think we should go find some grown-ups. I'm scared."

"Don't be scared. I'm here and nothing's going to happen."

Riley takes his sister by the hand and leads her to the door of the church. A plaque on the door reads *Santurio di San Damiano*. It takes both of them to push open the solid wood door. It must weigh a ton.

They enter into a small foyer where there is a small altar with a spindly crucifix hanging over it. Beside the altar is a small table with a basket that must be for donations, and beside the basket are some pamphlets. Riley sorts through them and finds one in English.

"This says San Damiano is the small church where Jesus spoke to Francis," Riley reads to his sister. "Remember Aunt Philomena told us about that this morning? In the big basilica she showed us the picture,

the fresco, of Saint Francis praying before the funny painted cross? Well, this is where that happened."

"It also says this is where Saint Clare started her convent, the Order of Poor Clares. She lived here until she died. Remember, Aunt Philomena pointed out the big Basilica of Saint Clare. Must be the same person . . . er, I mean saint."

Opening another door, Riley and Delaney find themselves inside a tiny chapel. It's nearly dark inside. A single ray of sunlight passes through the lone window and strikes the small altar and a painted crucifix. This crucifix is just like the one pictured in the fresco in the Basilica di San Francesco. Riley wonders if this is the very same crucifix that spoke to Saint Francis. Somehow he thinks it might talk to him too, and this makes him afraid.

A faint sound of someone sniffling comes from the back corner of the chapel. Riley looks over his shoulder and catches a glimpse of someone out of the corner of his eye. It's the man in the shabby green coat that he saw earlier – the same man who was sitting in front of the Basilica of Saint Clare – the one with eyes like the wolf's – the one with a rucksack.

A sense of panic passes through Riley. He grabs Delaney and pulls her through the nearest doorway.

A faint sound of someone sniffling comes from the back corner of the chapel.

They stumble through a series of small rooms, desperately looking for a way out. The rooms are nearly empty except for a few pieces of simple furniture. "I think this is where Saint Clare and the nuns lived."

"But where are the furniture and rugs?" asks Delaney.

"Maybe they didn't have any furniture. The pamphlet said they are called the 'Poor' Clares," says Riley.

After pushing on three different doors, they finally find one that opens. It leads them into an interior courtyard. There is a young nun in the courtyard tending to the flower garden. Without being noticed, Riley is able to jump up onto a low wall and can see the path that leads back to the park. He pulls Delaney up on the wall and together they jump onto the grass on the other side. From the inside of the courtyard comes a moaning sound, like the sound a wounded animal might make. Hand in hand Riley and Delaney race up the hill toward the park.

Riley's mind is racing as fast as his legs. Maybe the wolf led them to San Damiano to find the man with wolf-like eyes. Maybe the wolf and man are somehow united in spirit. Maybe the wolf wants them to help the man. Riley cannot quite make sense of it – but at least he knows that he's not imagining the wolf. Delaney saw it too!

SAINT CLARE

Riley and Delaney race across the road and enter the park just as Sister Philomena is finishing her prayers. She has no idea what these two have been up to, and it's probably better that way.

"Have you enjoyed your time in the park?" asks Sister Philomena.

"We followed the wolf!" exclaims Delaney.

Riley cringes as his little sister blurts out a confession. He knows their aunt will be very upset if she knows they left the park. Riley punches Delaney in the ribs to keep her from saying anything else.

"Ahh umm, we pretended a wolf led us to a secret place. Delaney exaggerates things sometimes," Riley says. He doesn't want to lie to his aunt, but he doesn't want to tell her about the wolf and the man – not just yet. "But we had a good time. This is a great park. When do we eat?" he asks, changing the subject.

"In about a half hour," says Sister Philomena, looking at her watch. "The Guest House serves a wonderful evening meal. Let's go get ready for dinner."

The meal at the Guest House was one of the best Riley remembers since he came to Italy. It started with a slice of melon wrapped in a slice of salty ham. Then they were served pasta with light cream sauce and chunks of cherry tomatoes. The salad was pretty ordinary, but good. The meat and vegetable dish consisted of grilled sausages and chunks of grilled vegetables all mixed together. Dessert was fresh strawberries with sweet whipped cream on top.

During dinner Riley wanted to tell Sister Philomena about their trip to San Damiano. He wanted to ask her about ghosts, spirits, and guardian angels to see if he could figure out a connection between the gray wolf and the gray man. However, there were other guests sitting with them in the dining room, and he didn't think it was appropriate to ask questions of Sister Philomena. So far no one there knew they were involved in the investigation at the basilica, and he felt sure his aunt wanted to keep it that way.

"Aunt Philomena, can you tell us more about Saint Francis and Saint Clare?" asks Riley, as his aunt tucks the children into their beds at the Guest House.

"I can't think of a more fitting way to end this very long and exciting day," says Sister Philomena.

"We talked a lot about Saint Francis when we studied the frescos in the basilica. But the friendship between Francis and Clare is important.

"Saint Clare was also born into a wealthy family in Assisi. She was about eleven years younger than Francis. Her family lived in a house just off the Piazza San Rufino. That is very near where we had the *gelato* earlier today.

"Clare was a very special and spiritual girl. She showed great devotion to the Lord at a very early age. Because they were from the same town, she knew Francis and admired his devotion to all of God's creation. Mostly she was impressed by his ability to give up every single possession and turn his life over to God.

"Clare wanted to follow in Francis's footsteps, but her father had other plans. He wanted his beautiful daughter to marry, and had even picked out a husband for her. Clare defied her father. She did not want to marry. She wanted to spend her life in prayer and adoration of the Lord. As time went on, Clare spent as much time as possible with Francis and the friars. They helped Clare to devise a plan to spend her life as she wished.

"It was on Palm Sunday when Clare was sixteen –

she escaped from her father's protective custody in Assisi and ran down the hill to the little Church of Santa Maria of the Portiuncola. Francis and some of the other friars were there waiting for her. They helped her to fend off her father and other relatives who were trying to get her to come back home. With the friars' help she cut her beautiful long hair and did away with her fancy clothes. They gave her a simple tunic to wear and she was very happy.

"It wasn't long before Clare was joined by her sister Agnes and friend Pacifica. In fact, within a few years, the Poor Clares had grown in number to over 300 sisters.

"Francis and the other friars built the sisters a convent at San Damiano and that's where they spent their life in prayer."

"Riley, is that where the wolf took us today?" asks a sleepy Delaney.

Sister Philomena looks at Delaney, trying to figure out what she might mean by that. Riley looks at her and shrugs his shoulders, as if to say "Kids, what do they know?"

Sister Philomena continues with her story. "Today, the Poor Sisters of Saint Clare are an order of nuns that live and pray both at the convent of San Damiano and the Basilica of Saint Clare, where my

*"With the friars' help she cut her beautiful long hair and
did away with her fancy clothes."*

good friend Sister Frances Marie is now the abbess. We'll meet her in the morning. Besides the sisters here in Assisi, there are over 20,000 Poor Clare Sisters in more than seventy-five countries around the world.

"There are stories of many miracles performed by Clare," says Sister Philomena, pointing to a statue of Saint Clare sitting on the bedside table. "Often, if the sisters were ill, Clare would pray over them and they would get better. Once one of the friars was very ill with a high fever. Not knowing what else to do, the brothers brought him to see Clare. She laid her hands on him and prayed. Almost immediately he became well again."

"I love Saint Clare," says Delaney, giving a big yawn. "But her house needs furniture and pictures. Can we talk more tomorrow? I have to sleep now." And with that Delaney closes her eyes and falls asleep.

"Riley, why is Delaney bringing up information about San Damiano and the wolf?" asks Sister Philomena.

Realizing that it is wrong to lie, and then realizing he will feel better if he tells his aunt what they did today, Riley unloads. He tells of seeing the wolf in various places in Assisi, of the look in the wolf's eyes, about the look in the man's eyes, about the trip to San Damiano and seeing the man in the chapel, and how he thinks it is all tied to the break-in at the basilica.

"Do you think the wolf could be sent by God to lead us to the answer? Or do you think it could be the thief's guardian angel trying to lead us to him? Or am I imagining things?" asks Riley.

"Well, Riley, I really don't know," says Sister Philomena. "You do have an active imagination, but you did experience some of those things. Let's wait until tomorrow and see what the investigators have learned. The facts of the investigation should tell if there is any connection."

ANOTHER CLUE!

Riley is awakened by the smell of sausage cooking and the sight of morning sunlight streaming through the slats of the shuttered windows. "Do I smell real food?" he asks.

Sister Philomena and Delaney are sitting side by side at a little table on the balcony to their room. Delaney has been drawing pictures of the angels she saw yesterday. Sister is amazed at the little girl's eye for detail and ability to draw.

"Yes," announces Delaney. "This place serves 'American breakfast,' not that boring old bread and cheese we eat at the convent. Come, I'll show you."

Delaney leads Riley to the Guest House dining room where he finds a buffet table filled with pots of scrambled eggs, fried potatoes, bacon, sausage, biscuits, fruit, cookies, and just about every kind of juice. "Aunt Philomena and I already ate. She says breakfast comes with the room, so eat up!"

Most hotels in Italy provide free breakfast if you stay there overnight. Seldom do you find one that provides an "American breakfast" with this selection eggs and hot meats. Riley decides detective work makes him hungry.

Riley is contemplating a second helping when his sister and aunt come to get him.

"Time to get back to work!" announces Sister Philomena. "Let's leave some food for the other guests," she teases. "We're going to stop by and see my old and dear friend, Sister Frances Marie, on the way back to the crime scene. She's the abbess of the Order of Poor Clares and has an office at the Basilica di Santa Chiara. Remember, we passed by it yesterday?"

Riley not only remembers the basilica, but he also remembers the man sitting beside it. The man that looked like a beggar but wasn't begging – the man with the eyes of the wolf.

"Buon Giorno!" The nun sitting at the reception desk just inside the entrance to the Basilica di Santa Chiara greets Sister Philomena and the children. She seems a little surprised to see two children trailing behind Sister Philomena, but Philomena is often full of surprises.

Riley and Delaney are wide-eyed as they enter

*She seems a little surprised to see two children trailing
behind Sister Philomena.*

yet another big church. This church is much plainer
than the others. Riley remembers that Aunt Philomena
called these the "poor" sisters. Maybe they cannot
afford pictures on their walls.

"So nice to see you. Please, follow me and I will
take you to Sister Frances Marie, the abbess."

Sister Frances Marie, who walks with a cane,
gives them a warm greeting and leads them into her
little office. It has stone walls, a stone floor, and a tiny
window. Although it looks cold, it actually feels quite
warm.

"What brings you all the way to Assisi?" asks
Sister Frances Marie. "Are we a hot spot for crime?"
Riley is impressed, and looks up at his aunt with a
sense of pride. Everyone in Italy must know his aunt,
the nun and famous crime investigator.

"I'm surprised you haven't heard," responds
Sister Philomena. "Although so far we have kept it
from the media, I thought news may have spread
through the grapevine here in Assisi."

Sister Philomena tells her friend all about the
events at the Basilica di San Francesco. About the
break-in, the theft of the silver stand that held the
precious works of Saint Francis, and how the children
found the Chartula.

"Sister Philomena, I may have a suspect in your theft!" says a wide-eyed Sister Frances Marie.

"There is a strange little man who has come to me because his daughter wants to join the Order of the Poor Clares. He has been here several times. Each time he asks how much it costs to join the Order. I try to explain that we do not charge for entry into the Sisters of Poor Clares. If a family can donate some money to help run the convent, that is all we ask. We are a contemplative order, as you know. We pray and fast – fast and pray. We don't need much to live on. The donations we receive from people visiting the basilica are sufficient."

"So why do you suspect this strange man has something to do with the crime at the Basilica di San Francesco?" asks Sister Philomena.

"Yesterday when he came to see me, the strange little man said he would bring his daughter here tonight to enter the order as a novice, to see if she is made for this life. He told me that he will donate something for her like a dowry; something he believes to be of great value. I told him the dowry was not necessary, but he insists.

"I think he is very poor," continues Sister Frances Marie. "Sometimes I see him sitting in the *piazza* here in front of the basilica, eating a simple sandwich which he takes from his rucksack. He often drinks wine from one of those little boxes."

Riley's ears start to burn, his throat tightens, and the breakfast he just ate sits like a lump in his stomach. He looks at his aunt, then asks her friend. "Does he use a straw to drink the wine, like for juice boxes?"

"I do believe he does," says Sister Frances Marie. "Is that important?"

"Does he look like a beggar in a shabby clothes?" questions Riley.

"Truly, he does," laughs Sister Frances Marie. "That is a good way to describe him. What are you thinking?"

"Have you seen a wolf around here lately, or even heard one howling in the night?" he asks.

"Well, no, can't say that I have. But then I might not know a wolf if it bit me. I will ask the other sisters. Perhaps someone down at the San Damiano sanctuary has heard something," says Sister Frances Marie.

She thinks to herself for a moment. "Wait. Now I remember. One of the novices was in the San Damiano courtyard yesterday afternoon and she did hear a strange sound. She said it was mournful, and

"Have you seen a wolf around here lately?" he asks.

that it almost sounded sorrowful – like an animal in pain. But when she looked, she didn't find any wounded animal."

Sister Philomena looks at her nephew with surprise and a sense of wonder and pride. He is observant and thinks like a detective – a good detective!

"Before we jump to any conclusions, let's meet this strange man and ask a few questions. What time will he be here?" asks Sister Philomena.

"About five this afternoon. Please, come back then. I am somewhat afraid to confront him on my own," says Sister Frances Marie.

While they wait for five o'clock to roll around, Sister Philomena and the children walk back to the Basilica of Saint Francis and meet with the *polizia* and *carabinieri* who have been working on the crime investigation.

"So far no matches on the fingerprints or DNA from the cells found on the straw," reports the senior investigator. "Perhaps this thief is very careful. Or perhaps it is his first crime. If he had committed a

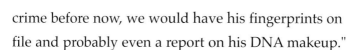

crime before now, we would have his fingerprints on file and probably even a report on his DNA makeup."

"Thank you, but please keep trying," encourages Sister Philomena. She looks through some of the reports. The investigative work is good. They even sent out inquiries to the nearby towns to see if anyone tried to sell or pawn a silver stand.

"Aunt Philomena?" Riley whispers. "Aren't you going to tell him about the Poor Sisters and the strange man and the wolf?"

Pulling Riley and Delaney out of earshot of the investigators, Sister Philomena explains. "Not right now. I am afraid Sister Frances Marie may be leading us astray – innocently, of course. I want to be sure. Besides, if these investigators think we have a suspect, they may jump in too fast and scare the man away. I prefer to wait until after the five o'clock appointment."

THE THIEF

A little before five o'clock, Sister Philomena, Riley and Delaney arrive at the Basilica of Saint Clare. Sister Philomena wants to show them something of importance before they meet with Sister Frances Marie.

Just inside the front door to the basilica and off to the right lies a small chapel. Inside there is a peculiar-looking wooden crucifix suspended from the ceiling. It looks a lot like the crucifix they saw in the big Basilica of Saint Francis and in the little chapel at San Damiano, only much older.

Sister Philomena whispers to them, "That crucifix hanging over the altar is the same crucifix from which Jesus spoke to Saint Francis over 800 years ago. Jesus asked Francis to dedicate his life to bringing people to faith. Francis accepted His calling.

Although Saint Francis lived a very poor and simple life, he is responsible for bringing more people to the faith than almost any other saint. He has had a profound influence on the world."

Bong. Bong. Bong. Bong. Bong. The intruding bell tolls not once, not twice, but five times.

"That's the five o'clock bell. Let's go, children. We may be able to solve a crime tonight," says Sister Philomena as she leads them through a side door and down a long hallway to a room adjoining the office of Sister Frances Marie.

Opening the door a crack, standing one above the other like heads on a totem pole, they strain to see and hear. "Be very quiet," Sister says. "Let's pretend we are statues!" They all giggle.

There's a knock at Sister Frances Marie's front office door. "*Avanti!*," she replies. "Come in, please."

A strange little man in a raggedy green coat and gray trousers enters her office. With him is a beautiful young woman. The rucksack in his hand looks to have something heavy inside.

Riley cannot see the man's face from where he is crouching – the tabletop is in his way. But he sees the rucksack and has a feeling it's the same man he saw on the street – the one with wolf-like eyes. His aunt is leaning so heavily on him that he cannot stand up any more. He listens.

"Please, good sister, my name is Luigi. I present my daughter, Elena. She wants to become a *clarissa*, a Sister of Saint Clare. But I don't want her and you to be so poor. So I offer you this silver stand of great value."

Sister Frances Marie nervously takes the rucksack from the strange little man. Is it what she thinks it is? She looks inside. It's covered with crumbs and is sticky from wine, but it looks like the silver stand that Sister Philomena said was stolen.

"Sister Philomena, please come in here!" she says excitedly, as she drops the sack to the floor. She is too nervous to keep hold of it.

All of a sudden, Sister Philomena and the two children burst through the side door.

"Stay where you are, and do not move," Sister Philomena directs the strange little man. "You too," she says to his confused-looking daughter. Sister is holding one hand out, as if to stop them from fleeing. She is rapidly punching in numbers on her cell phone with the other hand.

"Did we catch the thief?" shouts Delaney excitedly.

"Quiet," says Riley. He drags Delaney back flat against the wall beside him and puts his hands over her eyes and mouth.

"It's him! It's him! It's the man I saw on the street," announces Riley.

The sad little man begins to cry, falls to his

knees, and bows up and down, wailing and sobbing. *"Mi dispiace. Mi dispiace."*

"I just wanted to give you something of value to help the Poor Clares. I have been poor all my life. I wanted my beautiful daughter, my only living relative, to be happy, but not poor. But she insists on joining this convent, the poor sisters' convent. I thought if you had this beautiful silver stand, you might no longer be such poor nuns."

Sister Philomena puts her hand down. She realizes this man is not a real criminal and is not much of a threat. "Riley, pick up the bag and bring it to me, please," says Sister Philomena.

He does as asked. He peeks inside and shouts, "Yes! It's a silver stand!"

Just then three uniformed *polizia* and two *carabinieri* arrive at the office door. Sister Philomena had called them on her cell phone just in case she needed backup.

They rush in, take hold of the little man, and are ready to haul the thief away and lock him up.

"Please, please – not so fast," begs Sister Philomena. "Can Sister Frances Marie and I have a few minutes with this man?"

"Certo, of course Sister. Whatever you want. Do

The sad little man begins to cry, falls to his knees, and bows up and down, wailing and sobbing.

be careful," the officers caution, and leave to wait just outside the door to the small office.

The sisters question the man for a while. He has stopped sobbing and wailing, but is still crying. He tells them he is very sorry for the crime. He explains his motive again: it's to make his daughter happy and the Poor Clares less poor. He knows it is wrong to steal, and knows that he will be punished.

"Soon my daughter will be with the nuns, if they will still accept her. I have no other family and no work. I might as well go to jail," sobs the little man.

"What is your full name and where do you come from?" asks Sister Philomena. Based on Riley's observations, she suspects there is more mystery here than just a simple man breaking into the basilica and stealing.

"My full name is Luigi Lupo, and my family originates from Gubbio," sobs the little man.

Riley and Delaney look on in total amazement. It's as if their eyes are about to fall out of their sockets.

"Aunt Philomena, you said the Italian word for wolf is *lupo* – that's his last name! And he comes from Gubbio! That's where Saint Francis tamed the wild wolf! There has to be a connection!" exclaims Riley.

"My dear Riley, you are right. Perhaps the Holy Spirit used the wolf to lead us to Mr. Lupo. Perhaps when Mr. Lupo decided to commit a crime, his guardian angel left him and then went on to direct the wolf to lead us to him. Maybe somehow it's the spirit of the wolf of Gubbio paying back Saint Francis for saving his life so many years ago. We don't know how these things happen. But we do know that God works in mysterious ways, and He has answered our prayers.

The two nuns talk quietly for a short while, as the tearful daughter comforts her father.

"There may be an alternative to jail," says Sister Philomena to Luigi, the would-be thief. "Sister Frances Marie, the Abbess of the Poor Clares, tells me the convent is in need of a workman to help with heavy chores and repairs. Are you willing to help make restitution for this crime by working at the convent grounds? These sisters have a small shelter down the hill where you could sleep. They can send you some food daily. It won't be much, but it will be respectable. You will be near your daughter, but can only see her on special occasions. However, if you commit another crime, you will go to jail. Do you understand?"

Joy fills Luigi's heart. "Oh, yes. Never has anyone given me an opportunity such as this. I

"I will be a good and repentant man the rest of my life."

cannot believe that people can be so generous to such a poor, sinful, and sorrowful man as I am. I want to accept. But kind Sister, you and your nuns are poor, how can you afford to feed me and shelter me?"

"*Signore*," explains Sister Frances Marie, "we are poor only in that we do not own property. In our hearts we are very rich, because we know we have the love of God. He loves us and we love Him with all our hearts. We put our trust in Him and He provides for us. Your daughter will be rich with us."

"You will need to go with the officers to complete some paperwork," Sister Philomena tells Luigi. "But if it is all right with them and with Sister Frances Marie, you may return here to stay and to work. Just don't ever steal anything ever again. *Capite?*"

"*Si, Signora Sorella. Grazie. Grazie.* Thank you. Thank you. I will be a good and repentant man the rest of my life."

"Go in peace and joy. That's what Saint Francis would have said!"

THE END

Check out these other popular books from
Aunt Dee's Attic

Lost in Peter's Tomb

is the first book in the *Adventures with Sister Philomena, Special Agent to the Pope* series of mystery adventures. In Book One, Riley and Delaney rush to the Vatican with Sister Philomena to help the Pope with an intruder in the Apostolic Palace. A mischievous white cat leads them astray and they end up lost in Peter's tomb!

Retail Price $11.95

Today I Made My First Reconciliation

Best friends Maria and Riley accidentally break a window, then lie to their parents. Their growing discomfort coincides with encounters with their parish priests and teachers and lessons of forgiveness, love and reconciliation. Includes a "Guide to the Sacrament of Reconciliation" and memory book section.

*This book carries the imprimatur of the Catholic Church.

Retail Price $19.95

Today I Made My First Communion

Join Maria and Riley and their classmates as they offer to help Father Hugo solve the Mystery of the Eucharist. Learn about the Church, the Mass, music and prayer. "Look in the Back of the Book" for clues and information on the sacrament. A keepsake book to record the events of the day.

*This book carries the imprimatur of the Catholic Church.

Retail Price $19.95

Today I Was Baptized

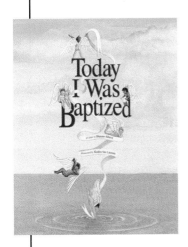

This charming book begins with a children's story about a baby's baptism day – told from the baby's perspective. Includes short essays that explain the sacrament of Baptism. The book becomes a keepsake for this very special day, allowing parents, godparents, and others to describe the day in the memory section in the back of the book. Makes a great gift!

*This book carries the imprimatur of the Catholic Church.

Retail Price $19.95

ITALIAN WORDS AND PHRASES

Whenever we travel to foreign places, it is nice to be able to converse with people in their own language. Even if we only can only speak a few words of their language, that alone lets our world neighbors know that we care about them and want to get to know them. Here are a few words and phrases that were used in this book and that Riley and Delaney might have learned in this adventure.

Italian Word	English Meaning
Andiamo	Let's go or hurry up
Avanti!	Come in!
Basilica	A big church built according to a specific architectural design that forms a cross
Capite?	Do you understand?
Carabinieri	The army police who maintain order
Ciao	Hello or goodbye (a general friendly greeting)
Cittá	City or town
Certo!	Certainly!
Custode	Caretaker or custodian
Directtore	Director
Fratello/Sorella	Brother/Sister
Gelato	Italian ice cream
Giardino	Garden
Grazie	Thank you
Mangiare	Eat
Mi dispiace	I am sorry
Oh, Dio mio	Oh, my God (said as a prayer)
Oliva	Olive
Padre/Madre	Father/Mother
Parco	Park
Pastore	Shepherd
Piazza	Public square or cental point in the city
Polizia	The civil police who investigate crimes
Pronto	Ready (used when answering a telephone)
Rapidamente!	Quickly!
San Francesco	Saint Francis
Santa Chiara	Saint Clare
Si	Yes
Signora/Signorina	Madam or Mrs./Miss or young lady
Signore	Sir or mister
Tabacchi	A type of convience store
Venuto qui	Come here
Vigneto	Vineyard
Zia / Zio	Aunt / Uncle

Animali
(Animals):

Italian . . .	English
cane	dog
cavallo	horse
cúcciolo	puppy
gattino	kitten
gatto	cat
lupo	wolf
maiale	pig
mucca	cow
pecora	sheep
pesce	fish

Transporto
(Transportation):

Italian . . .	English
autobus	bus
a cavallo	horseback
aeroplano	airplane
treno	train
macchina	car
metro	subway
motoscafo	motorboat
motoretta	motor scooter
carrozza	carriage
taxi	taxi

Insetti e cose
(Bugs and things):

Italian . . .	English
calabrone	bumblebee
formica	ant
pipistrello	bat
ragno	spider
rana	frog
rospo	toad
serpente	snake
verne	worm
vespa	wasp

Alimenti favoriti
(Favorite foods):

Italian . . .	English
spaghetti e polpette	spaghetti and meatballs
biscotti e latte	cookies and milk
panino	sandwich
ciccolato caldo	hot chocolate
zuppa	soup
pizza con formaggio	pizza with cheese
caramella	candy
patatine fritto	French fries
coca	Coke®